Acknowledgements

For
My parents, who teach me.
Dr. Rachita Dhurat, who guides me.
My wife and kids Dr Minal Mishra, Vedant and Adhyan,
who inspire me.

HAIR TODAY, GONE TOMORROW RESTORE NOW!!

"THE HAIRLINE HUSTLE"

DR. SUNIL MISHRA

Made with ❤ on the Notion Press Platform
www.notionpress.com

Contents

Introduction

You never realize how much you love your hair until it starts to leave you.

Seriously. Think about it. When was the last time you looked in the mirror and truly *appreciated* your hair? For most people, it's just there, sitting on top of your head, doing its thing. You comb it, wash it, maybe throw some gel or mousse in it if you're feeling fancy, and go about your day. Hair is like a background character in the movie of your life always there, never really noticed, but quietly playing a supporting role.

But the minute it starts disappearing? Oh, boy. That's when the drama starts.

For Aryan (our hero of this little story), hair loss wasn't something he ever thought about until it became something he couldn't stop thinking about. He went from carefree, wind-in-his-hair confidence to full-blown panic the day he noticed his hairline was starting to... retreat.

And trust me, Aryan didn't take it well.

Let's rewind for a second. Imagine this: You're in your late twenties. You've got a solid job, a decent social life, and a hairline that's been with you since your teenage years, never letting you down. Life is good. You're not exactly Shahrukh Khan, but you're not *not* Shahrukh Khan either. In other words, you've got it together hair included.

But one day, you're getting ready for work, glancing in the mirror as you brush your teeth, and you notice something. Is it just you, or does your forehead look a little... bigger? You blink. You lean in closer. And that's when you see it: your hairline. It's not where it used to be. In fact, it's slowly but surely taking a step back, like it's planning a strategic retreat.

Cue the existential crisis.

That's exactly what happened to Aryan. One minute, he was living his life, blissfully unaware of the slow-motion hair exodus happening on his scalp. The next minute, he was spiraling into a full-blown panic, frantically Googling things like "how to regrow hair overnight" and "why is my hairline betraying me?" Spoiler alert: there are no quick fixes, and yes, genetics can be cruel.

Hair Today, Gone Tomorrow

Hair loss is one of those things that no one talks about until it happens to them. And when it does? Oh boy, the floodgates open. Suddenly, you're hyper-aware of every strand you lose in the shower, every thinning spot on your crown, every reflection that catches you at a bad angle. It's like your hairline becomes the star of a horror movie, slowly creeping backward while you scream, "Nooooooo!" And here's the kicker: it doesn't happen all at once. Hair loss is like that friend who "drops by for a minute" but ends up staying for hours. It sneaks in slowly, quietly, until one day you wake up and realize that your hair isn't where you left it. For Aryan, this realization hit hard. He was used to being the guy with the thick, wavy hair, the guy who could roll out of bed, run a hand through his hair, and be good to go. But now? Now he was the guy who was spending way too much time in the bathroom, inspecting his hairline from every possible angle, wondering where it all went wrong. What made it worse? No one tells you that hair loss is basically a team effort. It's not just genetics, though they play a starring role, it's the epigenetics, stress, diet, lifestyle, pollution, infection, hormones and sometimes, just plain bad luck. And Aryan? Aryan was about to learn that lesson the hard way.

Who Invited Genetics to This Party?

Let's talk about **genetics** for a second. Genetics is that party guest who shows up uninvited, drinks all the good wine, and refuses to leave, even after you've dropped enough hints to make it clear they're not welcome. In Aryan's case, genetics was the main culprit behind his hair loss and it didn't care about his feelings. See, Aryan's family tree wasn't exactly known for its lush foliage. His dad had been bald for as long as Aryan could remember, and his grandpa? Let's just say he'd been rocking the shiny dome look since the 70s. But Aryan had always assumed *hoped* that he'd dodged the genetic bullet. After all, his mom had thick, curly hair well into her 50s, and Aryan figured he must have inherited her side of the family's hair genes. But genetics doesn't play favorites. It doesn't care that Aryan had gotten comfortable with his hair. It had its own plans and those plans didn't include a full head of hair for Aryan.

Stress: The Ultimate Barber

But genetics wasn't the only player in this game. No, Aryan's lifestyle wasn't exactly doing him any favors either. The thing about hair loss is that it's not just about what's happening on top of your head it's about what's happening in your life. And Aryan's life? Well, let's just say it wasn't the picture of relaxation. Work deadlines, late night calls, endless emails, lack of sleep, and the occasional existential crisis about the meaning of life, it all added up. And according to the internet (which is never wrong, right?), stress was basically the equivalent of hiring a barber to shave off your hair, one strand at a time. Aryan had always considered himself a laid-back guy, but as the hair kept disappearing, he started to wonder if maybe just maybe he was a little more stressed out than he thought. After all, it wasn't just his hairline that was retreating his sleep, his energy, and his sense of calm were all packing their bags and joining the exodus.

The Hair-Care Rabbit Hole

Then came the rabbit hole of **hair-care products**. If you've never fallen into the abyss of online hair-loss solutions, consider yourself lucky. It's a world full of miracle serums, questionable supplements, and shampoos that promise to regrow your hair faster than you can say "biotin." And Aryan? Aryan tried them all. The oils, the scalp massages, the serums that smelled like a tropical rainforest but did nothing for his hairline Aryan went through the whole catalog of products, hoping that one of them would be the magic bullet. Spoiler: there was no magic bullet. But there *was* a lot of greasy pillowcases and frustration.

Letting Go: The Real Journey Begins

As Aryan's hairline continued its slow-motion retreat, he realized that maybe, just maybe, he was going about this whole thing the wrong way. Maybe the key wasn't to fight his hair loss tooth and nail. Maybe the key was to *accept* it or at least, stop letting it drive him crazy. And so began Aryan's journey. A journey of self-discovery, hair masks, meditation, morning walks, yoga classes (yes, really), and a few awkward encounters along the way. He learned that hair loss isn't the end of the world it's just another part of life. A part that can be managed with humor, some lifestyle tweaks, and a lot of deep breathing. Because here's the thing: hair loss might change the way you look, but it doesn't change *who you are*. And Aryan? Aryan was about to figure that out the hard way.

The Hair-Loss Survival Guide You Didn't Know You Needed

This book isn't your typical hair-loss guide. It's not full of medical jargon or "guaranteed" solutions that will magically grow your hair back overnight (because let's be honest, those don't exist). No, this book is about the reality of hair loss the awkwardness, the frustration, the occasional panic, and the eventual acceptance. And if you're reading this, chances are you've been where Aryan's been. You've looked in the mirror and wondered why your hairline is inching backward like it's trying to escape your face. You've googled "how to stop hair loss" at 3 a.m. and fallen down the rabbit hole of dubious solutions. You've probably even considered shaving your head entirely, just to take control of the situation. But here's the thing: you're not alone. Hair loss is a universal experience, and it's one that can be tackled with humor, patience, and a little bit of trial and error.

So, buckle up. You're about to join Aryan (probably you too with the same experience) on a hair-raising adventure that's equal parts ridiculous, relatable, and believe it or not a little bit inspiring. Because if Aryan can survive hair loss with his sense of humor intact, you can too.

Welcome to the Hair Today Gone Tomorrow Restore Now!! "Hairline Hustle" . Let's get this journey started.

CHAPTER I

"Who Invited Genetics to This Party?"

There are some things in life you can control like what you eat for breakfast or what socks you wear. And then there are the things you *can't* control like which side of the family gifted you your receding hairline. Aryan had always been an optimist. The kind of guy who believed that with a little effort, most problems could be solved. Bad day at work? Pizza and Netflix. Rough night of sleep? Three cups of coffee would do the trick. But when it came to his hair, Aryan didn't realize that all the optimism in the world wouldn't stop the inevitable. You see, Aryan was under the impression that he could outsmart his genetics. It wasn't that he was *totally* unaware of his family's bald history he knew, deep down, that it was lurking. But like most people who are blissfully ignorant, Aryan convinced himself that *he* would be different. His hair wouldn't follow the family tradition. He had things like modern science, better shampoo, better serums, social media !! and, most importantly, *hope* on his side.

Unfortunately for Aryan, genetics doesn't care about your shampoo choices or your hope.

**The Early Warning Signs:
Ignorance is Bliss (Until It Isn't)**

For most of his life, Aryan had a pretty solid head of hair. Thick, wavy, and always slightly tousled in that "I woke up like this" kind of way, Aryan's hair had never been a source of concern. In fact, it was one of his best features. People often complimented him on it, and he had never had to put much effort into keeping it looking good. If there was one thing Aryan could count on, it was that his hair would always have his back (or, more accurately, his head). But as he reached his late 20s, Aryan started to notice something strange. Nothing drastic just a subtle shift in the way his hair behaved. It wasn't as thick as it used to be. When he ran his fingers through it, it didn't feel as full. And occasionally, after a shower, he'd find a few more hairs than usual circling the drain. At first, Aryan shrugged it off. "No big deal," he told himself. "Everybody loses hair. Stress, bad diet, late night calls, sleep who knows? It'll bounce back." Aryan's go-to solution for everything was optimism. He figured that if he ignored the problem long enough, it would go away on its own. But it didn't go away. In fact, it got worse. Slowly, almost imperceptibly, Aryan's hairline started to inch backward, like it was retreating in the face of some invisible enemy. His once-perfectly positioned hairline was now starting to take up real estate that used to belong to his forehead. And yet, even as the signs were becoming clearer, Aryan stayed in denial. "It's just a bad hair week," he said, smoothing down the thinning spots. "Maybe I'm just stressed out. Or maybe it's the lighting in here." Because denial? Denial was *comfortable*. Denial didn't force Aryan to confront the fact that he might be turning into his dad or worse, his *grandpa*.

The Family Tree: Bald Branches Everywhere

Here's the thing about Aryan's family: they weren't exactly known for their luscious locks. His dad had been bald since Aryan could remember rocking the classic horseshoe of hair around the sides of his head and not much else. And his grandpa? Well, let's just say he had ditched the idea of hair decades ago and was sporting a shine on top that could rival the sun. But Aryan had always assumed *hoped* that he had inherited his mother's genes. His mom, bless her, still had a full head of hair in her 50s, as did most of her side of the family. Aryan would look at his mom's thick, curly hair and think, *That's where I get it from. Not Dad's side. No way.* For years, Aryan had been walking around under the assumption that genetics was playing favorites, and he was on the winning team. Even when his dad made little jokes about "joining the club" or "better get used to hats," Aryan brushed it off.

"That's your side of the family," Aryan would say confidently. "I got Mom's hair."

To which his dad would just shake his head and mutter something about "just you wait."

But then, *it happened*. The day Aryan had to face the cold, hard truth about his genetics. It was a Saturday morning, and Aryan was getting ready to go out with some friends. He was brushing his hair in the bathroom, minding his own business, when he noticed something...off. He leaned in closer to the mirror, squinting at his hairline. There it was. The truth staring back at him. It was subtle, but unmistakable *a thinning patch*. A spot near the front where his hair wasn't as thick as it used to be. Aryan stared at it for a long time, as if by sheer force of will, he could make it go away. But it didn't go away. It was real. Aryan's heart sank. His mind started racing. "This can't be happening," he muttered. "Maybe it's just the lighting. Or maybe I'm just tired. Yeah, that's it I'm tired." But deep down, Aryan knew what was happening.

Genetics had just RSVP'd to the party.

The Six Stages of Hair Loss Denial

Aryan's descent into hair loss wasn't immediate. It was a slow, gradual process that could only be described as a twisted version of the six stages of grief.

1. Denial: "It's just a phase. My hair will bounce back. Everyone's hair looks a little thin under harsh lighting."

2. Anger: "Seriously, universe? I've got enough on my plate without losing my hair too! Why couldn't I get Mom's genes?!"

3. Bargaining: "Okay, look, I'll start eating healthier. I'll even drink spinach, carrots, apples and beetroot smoothies and quit eating pizza at midnight if that's what it takes. Just don't let me go bald."

4. Depression: "It's over. I'm going to look like my dad in five years. Hats are my future. I'll never have good hair again."

5. Acceptance: "Alright, fine. My hairline's on the run, but it's not the end of the world... yet."

6. Correcting and Preventing: "Ok its time to get to an expert dermatologist opinion for treating the hair loss and lifestyle modification to prevent further damage"

Of course, Aryan spent most of his time oscillating between denial and bargaining. He was determined to find a way to reverse the trend, to outsmart the genetics that were clearly plotting against him. But as the months went on, it became harder and harder to stay in denial. The signs were everywhere more hair in the drain, more forehead in the mirror, more comments from friends like "Hey, have you ever thought about growing a beard?"

The Balding Family Legacy: Like Father, Like Son

The more Aryan thought about it, the more he realized that he had been ignoring the inevitable for years. He had always known that his dad and grandpa had both lost their hair early in life, but he'd never let himself believe it could happen to *him*. He had spent most of his adult life acting like he was immune to the family curse, like somehow, he had dodged the genetic bullet. But now? Now it was clear: the bullet had hit him, and it was just taking its sweet time to fully sink in. Aryan remembered family gatherings where his dad and grandpa would sit around talking about how much money they'd saved on shampoo and haircuts. It was always good-natured, lighthearted teasing, but Aryan had never really been part of the conversation. He had his hair he was safe. Except now, as Aryan looked at his thinning hairline in the mirror, he realized that he was about to become the newest member of the Bald Brigade. He could already picture the next family reunion, where his dad would give him a knowing look and say, "Told you so, son." And Aryan? Well, he'd have to laugh it off, but inside, a little part of him would be mourning the loss of his once-glorious hairline.

Aryan's Last Stand: Trying to Outsmart Genetics

Even though Aryan knew, deep down, that genetics was behind his thinning hair, he wasn't ready to give up without a fight. This was his hairline, and he was going to do everything he could to defend it. So, Aryan started doing what any self-respecting person would do when faced with a problem they don't want to accept: he turned to the internet for solutions. Surely, there had to be something out there that could reverse the effects of genetics, right?

Aryan spent hours reading articles with titles like:

"How to Stop Genetic Hair Loss in Its Tracks"

"Top 10 Foods to Eat for Hair Regrowth"

"Can Yoga Save Your Hairline?"

"The Ultimate Hair Growth Guide: What Your Doctor Isn't Telling You"

It wasn't long before Aryan's browser history was a minefield of hair-loss remedies, from the sensible ("Use a gentle shampoo and conditioner!") to the utterly ridiculous ("Rub mashed potatoes, onion and garlic on your scalp twice a week!"). Aryan was willing to try anything, no matter how absurd it sounded. And try, he did. He started using hair products he'd never heard of, buying vitamins that promised to boost hair growth, and experimenting with scalp massages that supposedly "activated dormant follicles." Every night, Aryan would go through his elaborate routine, convinced that he was outsmarting his genetics one scalp massage at a time. But despite his efforts, the hairline retreat continued. Slowly, but surely, genetics was winning.

The Inevitable Acceptance

After months of trying to outwit his DNA, Aryan finally came to terms with the fact that genetics was playing the long game and it was winning. After all it was his father's genes , how can it not affect him? No matter how many products he used or how many scalp massages he gave himself, his hairline wasn't coming back. And while it wasn't completely gone, Aryan had to accept that it would never be what it once was. And you know what? That was okay. Because here's the thing: sometimes, life throws you a curveball. Sometimes, genetics pulls the rug (or in this case, the hair) out from under you. And no amount of optimism, denial, or weird internet remedies can change that. For Aryan, acceptance wasn't about giving up. It was about letting go of the idea that he had to control everything. Genetics had shown up to the party, whether Aryan liked it or not, and now it was time to find a new way forward. After all, hair may come and go, but Aryan? Aryan was still Aryan with or without a perfect hairline.

CHAPTER II

"Stress: The Ultimate Barber?"

After genetics which entered Aryan's party its the time for Stress. It's like the unexpected guest who shows up at your party, eats all the good snacks, and overstays their welcome. And for Aryan, it was the unwelcome barber who had snuck into his life, snipping away at his hairline one stress-filled day at a time. The thing is, Aryan wasn't the kind of guy who would have ever described himself as "stressed." No, he was the laid-back type *the guy who rolls with the punches*, the one who "doesn't sweat the small stuff." At least, that's what he *thought*. But what Aryan didn't realize was that stress wasn't the kind of enemy you could see coming. It didn't announce itself with a dramatic crash like the villain entering in the hero's life in a Bollywood styled movie or like a life-changing moment in someone's life. It crept in slowly disguised as long workdays, late-night emails, traffic jams, lack of sleep and one-too-many all-nighters fueled by coffee and questionable decisions. Stress was, as Aryan would soon learn, the ultimate stealth barber, and it was quietly doing more damage to his hairline than any bad shampoo, serum or questionable haircut ever could.

The Hairline That Wasn't Stressed, Until It Was

Aryan's descent into stress-induced hair loss started innocently enough. He was in his late 20s, a time when he was supposed to be at the peak of his physical and professional game. And on the surface, he was. He had a solid job as a manager in one of the MNC in Mumbai, a decent social life, good number of social media friend's who would like his post and no major crises to speak of. Sure, work had gotten a little more intense recently, but that was normal, right? He was just "busy," like everyone else. Except that "busy" had slowly transformed into "overwhelmed," and "overwhelmed" had morphed into a low-grade, ever-present sense of anxiety that Aryan had become so used to, he didn't even realize it was there anymore. And then, one morning, as Aryan stood in front of the bathroom mirror, bleary-eyed and still half-asleep, he saw it.

A bald spot. OMG !! or, more accurately, a *thin* spot.

It wasn't huge, but it was definitely there a patch near his crown where the hair wasn't quite as thick as it used to be. Aryan blinked, leaned in closer to the mirror, and examined it from every angle.

"Is that new? Has that always been there?" he muttered, his heart rate picking up.

He ran his fingers through his hair, hoping it was just bedhead or maybe bad lighting. But no the hair was thinner. Aryan's first thought was that it had to be a one-off situation. Maybe he'd slept on it funny. Or maybe it was just temporary stressful week, bad diet, nothing serious. Right?

Wrong.!!!

Stress: The Silent Scissor-Wielder

Here's the thing about stress: it's sneaky. It doesn't always show up with big, dramatic symptoms like a heart attack or a breakdown in the middle of a board meeting (though that happens too). No, sometimes stress just quietly chips away at you, little by little. And in Aryan's case, it was quietly chipping away at his hair. As Aryan's workdays stretched longer, his sleep got shorter. Emails were coming in at all hours, and for some reason, it seemed like every deadline was *yesterday*. His weekends were no longer about relaxing they were about catching up on all the work he didn't get to during the week. By the time Sunday night rolled around, Aryan felt like he was on a hamster wheel, running in place but getting nowhere. And with each passing day, more hair was starting to jump ship. At first, it was just a few extra strands in the shower drain. Then it was more hair on his pillow in the morning. Eventually, Aryan couldn't help but notice that his forehead seemed to be growing. The hairline wasn't just receding it was retreating, like it was trying to get as far away from his stressed-out scalp as possible. Of course, Aryan did what any rational person would do in his situation: *he ignored it.* "It's just a phase," he told himself. "Everyone loses hair when they're stressed, right? This will pass."

Except it didn't pass. In fact, it got worse.

Aryan's First Attempt at Stress Management: The Herbal Tea Disaster

When the hair loss didn't stop (and when his friends started making subtle comments like "You ever think about shaving your head, man? It could look cool!"), Aryan realized he had to do something. So, naturally, he turned to the internet. After several hours of Googling phrases like "how to stop stress hair loss" and "miracle stress remedies," Aryan stumbled upon something that seemed easy enough to try: **herbal tea**. According to the wellness bloggers of the world, herbal tea was a magical elixir that could calm your nerves, relax your body, and most importantly stop stress in its tracks. And, apparently, less stress meant less hair loss. It was perfect! Aryan rushed to the store and stocked up on every tea that promised to relax, restore, and rejuvenate. That night, Aryan brewed himself a giant mug of **chamomile tea** (the queen of calm, according to the internet) and settled into his couch, waiting for the magic to happen. He expected instant results like the tea would wash away all his worries, and maybe even stop his hair from falling out right then and there.

But as Aryan sat there, sipping his tea, he didn't feel relaxed. He felt... bored. "This is it?" he muttered, looking at the mug. "This is supposed to stop stress? Where's the magic?". Aryan couldn't feel any difference, so he made one more cup of his magic elixir. Still no effect!!. Finally after his third cup, Aryan felt more annoyed than anything. The only thing chamomile had done was make him need to pee. The next night, he tried **lavender tea**, which smelled nice but made him feel like he was drinking bathwater. By night three, Aryan had tried **peppermint tea**, which didn't calm him down at all but did make his breath minty fresh. Eventually, after trying for many nights with many variants of herbal tea, Aryan gave up on tea altogether. The only thing it had done was make him crankier and more convinced that stress-relief bloggers were con artists.

Aryan started cursing the social media experts for their nonsense quick fix advice.

The Yoga Fiasco: Aryan's First and Last Class

After the herbal tea disaster, Aryan decided to take a more active approach to managing his stress. If sitting around sipping tea wasn't going to cut it, maybe he needed to *move*. And what better way to de-stress than through the ancient practice of yoga? Aryan had always been vaguely aware of yoga, but he'd never actually considered doing it himself. Yoga, in Aryan's mind, was for people who wore stretchy pants and drank green juice for fun. It wasn't for guys like him, guys who preferred pizza and Netflix marathons to bending their bodies into pretzel-like shapes. But after reading several articles that swore by yoga's magical ability to reduce stress and *improve hair health* (yes, that's a real claim some people make), Aryan decided to give it a shot. But then there were so many variants of yoga- power yoga, beginners yoga, intense yoga etc etc... after a detailed discussion with his friends and close ones he signed up for a beginner's yoga class at a studio near his house. The instructor, a woman named Pallavi who had the kind of Zen calm that made Aryan feel instantly frazzled, welcomed him with a gentle smile. "Just relax," she said, "and let your body do the work."

Relax? Aryan was anything but relaxed.

The class started out simple enough just some light stretches and breathing exercises. Aryan could handle that. He felt nice about his body getting stretched. But then things took a turn. Suddenly, Pallavi was calling out pose names that sounded like they were part of some secret yoga language. *Downward dog, child's pose, warrior one, cobra*it all blurred together as Aryan tried to follow along. By the time they got to *tree pose*, Aryan's legs were shaking like he was trying to stand on a wobbly chair in a windstorm. He glanced around the room everyone else looked calm, serene, balanced. Meanwhile, Aryan was doing everything he could to avoid toppling over.

Then came *pigeon pose*, and that's when Aryan's body officially quit.

"Feel the stretch in your hips," Pallavi said calmly, her voice like honey.

Feel the stretch? Aryan felt like his entire body was being twisted into a human pretzel. By the time the class ended, Aryan was drenched in sweat, his muscles ached in places he didn't even know existed, and his mind was anything but calm.

Yoga, as it turned out, wasn't Aryan's thing.

Aryan Tries Meditation: The Great Mind Stillness Fail

After the yoga fiasco, Aryan figured that maybe he needed to go in the opposite direction. Less movement, more stillness. That's when he decided to try meditation. According to every self-help blog he could find, meditation was the ultimate stress-buster. All you had to do was sit still, breathe deeply, and let your mind relax. Simple enough, right? Aryan, the high tech IT guy downloaded a meditation app (because, of course, there's an app for that), put on some soothing nature sounds, and sat cross-legged on his living room floor. The app's voice guided him through the process: "Close your eyes. Breathe in deeply. Breathe out. Now, let go of your thoughts. Empty your mind." Aryan tried. He really did. But about two minutes into the session, his mind was anything but empty.

Did I forget to send that email? I think I forgot to send that email. What if an asteroid hits earth ? Can there be aliens sitting on the asteroid and attack humanity !!.Wait, why does my foot feel numb? Is that normal? Is this how you're supposed to sit? Maybe I should check if there's a better meditation position. Crap, I opened my eyes. Am I supposed to open my eyes? What if I can't get my foot feeling back? Can you lose a foot from bad meditation? I should Google that.

By the time the guided meditation was over, Aryan had managed to think about everything on earth and around the solar-system *except* letting go of his thoughts. Meditation, as it turned out, was harder than it looked.

Aromatherapy: The scent of desperation

After the disaster of meditation, Aryan was a bit of disappointed . Nothing was really working for him. So when his colleague Tanisha suggested aromatherapy, he thought, "Why not? If it doesn't grow hair, at least my head will smell like a fancy candle."

So there he was, in a dimly lit room with whale sounds playing in the background. A woman who introduced herself as "Moonbeam" gently guided Aryan to lie down on a massage table, his head positioned directly under a misty diffuser. "These essential oils will awaken the follicles, release stress, and invite positive hair energy," she said, waving a bottle of lavender oil like it was some magical potion.

As Moonbeam rubbed a concoction of lavender, rosemary, and peppermint oil on his scalp, Aryan couldn't help but wonder if he was marinating for a barbecue. But as the scent filled the room, Aryan felt... oddly at peace. The stress of his thinning hair seemed to float away like a loose strand in the wind. For a moment, he even imagined his hair sprouting back as thick as a lion's mane.

Then came the surprise. Moonbeam lit an herbal-infused candle, leaned in closer, and whispered, "Now we let the oils work their magic." She left the room, leaving Aryan to "absorb the healing."

Five minutes passed. Ten. Fifteen. Soon Aryan was snoring. And just as he hit the deepest part of his nap, a drop of oil from the diffuser landed on his forehead. Startled awake, Aryan jerked up, knocking over the candle. In a chaotic flurry, Moonbeam burst in to rescue the situation, while Aryan frantically patted his head to make sure nothing was on fire.

In the end, Aryan left the aromatherapy session with a relaxed mind, a sweet-smelling scalp, and exactly the same amount of hair he'd walked in with. But for those 30 minutes, he hadn't worried about his hair at all.

"Well, at least now I smell like a meadow," he thought as he left, slightly poorer but oddly uplifted.

Aromatherapy might not give you a thick head of hair, but it might give you a thick moment of peace. Plus, you'll smell like a spa brochure. Not a bad trade-off.

Aryan's Final Attempt: The Stress Ball Meltdown

At this point, Aryan had tried herbal teas, yoga, meditation, and even a brief (and ill-fated) experiment with aromatherapy (he'd read that lavender oil was supposed to calm you down, but all it did was make his head smell like a spa, which just made him feel weird about watching *Game of Thrones* with lavender in the air). So, in a moment of desperation, Aryan turned to the one stress-relief technique he hadn't yet tried: *the stress ball.* It seemed so simple. You just squeeze it. That's it. There was no fancy ritual, no guided breathing, no complex poses. Just a squishy little ball you could clench whenever you felt the need to strangle someone. For the first day, Aryan carried the stress ball around everywhere. At work, during meetings, while answering emails it became his new best friend. And for a while, it seemed to help. Every time Aryan felt his stress levels rising, he squeezed the ball like it owed him money. But then, during one particularly stressful day at work, Aryan's stress ball met its demise. His boss had just dumped a last-minute project on his desk, and Aryan, already frazzled, reached for his stress ball and squeezed it with all his might. That's when the ball burst. Right there, in the middle of his office. Aryan was left sitting at his desk, staring at the now-deflated, useless lump of foam in his hand, feeling more stressed than ever.

"That's it," Aryan muttered to himself. "I give up. Stress wins."

The Realization: You Can't Stress About Stress (Or Hair)

It wasn't until Aryan hit stress-ball rock bottom that he finally had an epiphany. Maybe just maybe the problem wasn't that he needed to find the *perfect* stress-relief technique. Maybe the problem was that he was trying too hard to control everything. He was stressing out about being stressed, and in the process, stressing out even more about his hair loss. And here's the funny thing about stress: the more you fight it, the worse it gets. So, instead of trying to force himself into a Zen-like state with yoga and meditation, Aryan decided to take a different approach. He let go. Not in the "everything is fine, I'm perfectly calm" way, but in the "okay, so life is stressful sometimes, and that's fine" way. Aryan accepted that stress was going to be a part of life, there was no magic tea or perfect meditation that was going to make it disappear. But what he *could* do was stop letting it control him. And once he stopped obsessing over stress, he stopped obsessing over his hair loss, too.

The Hairline That Stayed (Mostly) in Place

And wouldn't you know it? Once Aryan stopped stressing about his stress, his hairline stopped retreating quite so fast. It wasn't a miracle cure, but by focusing less on the problem, Aryan gave his body (and his scalp) a chance to recover. His hair wasn't growing back in thick, luscious waves, but the shedding had slowed down. He even felt like his hair looked a little healthier maybe it was the yoga, maybe it was the herbal tea, or maybe it was just the fact that Aryan wasn't freaking out every time he saw a few stray hairs in the shower. In the end, Aryan realized that stress wasn't just the ultimate barber, it was also the ultimate *test*. The more he stressed about losing his hair, the more hair he lost. But when he let go, when he accepted that some things were out of his control, he found the balance he'd been searching for.

CHAPTER III

"The Lifestyle of the Follicle-ly Challenged"

If genetics was the unwanted guest that showed up uninvited to Aryan's hair loss party, then his *lifestyle choices* were the ones sending out the invitations. Of course, Aryan didn't realize that at first. He had always assumed that his love of fast food, his aversion to exercise, and his late-night Netflix marathons couldn't possibly affect his hair. Hair loss was a genetic thing, right?

Wrong.

As it turns out, the way you treat your body can have a *huge* impact on your hair. And Aryan's body? Well, it was starting to show the signs of years of abuse. His diet was less "balanced" and more "pizza in one hand, coffee in the other." Exercise? Only if you count sprinting to catch the bus. Sleep? Who needs that when there's a new season of his favorite show to binge? But after months of watching his hairline recede faster than he could finish a cheeseburger, Aryan began to wonder if his lifestyle might have something to do with it. And so began his journey into the strange, confusing, and often hilarious world of *healthy living*.

Aryan's First Attempt at Healthy Eating:
The Spinach-Banana Smoothie Disaster

Let's start with the obvious: Aryan wasn't a fan of vegetables and fruits. Sure, he could handle the occasional side of fries (which, as far as Aryan was concerned, counted as a vegetable), but leafy greens? Spinach? And fruits like banana? Those were foreign concepts. But according to every health blog Aryan read, a good diet was essential for hair health. "Feed your body, feed your follicles," one particularly enthusiastic article had said. Apparently, foods rich in vitamins and minerals could help slow down hair loss and even promote regrowth. Aryan wasn't sure how much he believed that, but he was desperate enough to try. So, one Saturday morning, Aryan marched into his local grocery store and stocked up on all the "superfoods" he could find: spinach, bananas, avocados, chia seeds, pumpkin seeds and something called *flaxseed* that he wasn't quite sure what to do with. The cashier gave him an approving nod as he bagged his groceries, which only made Aryan more determined to become the picture of health. That afternoon, Aryan decided to make himself a **spinach-banana smoothie**. How hard could it be? After all, Ankita was always raving about her morning smoothies, and she had great hair. Maybe this was the key. Aryan tossed a handful of spinach into the blender, threw in a banana (because why not?), added some cinnamon and ginger, blended the whole thing into a green, goopy mess. He took a deep breath, poured the concoction into a glass, and took his first sip. It was...disgusting. Aryan gagged. "How does anyone drink this?" he muttered, eyeing the remaining smoothie like it was toxic waste. It tasted like dirt, with a side of disappointment. Aryan knew healthy eating was supposed to be good for you, but was it supposed to taste *this* bad? Still, Aryan wasn't one to give up after one failure. He made a few adjustments more banana, less spinach, a splash of almond milk and tried again. The result? Slightly less disgusting, but still very much *disgusting*. After a few more failed smoothie experiments, Aryan decided that maybe the health bloggers were lying. Spinach smoothies weren't the answer to hair loss. In fact, they were probably part of the problem.

Aryan's Brief (and Painful) Foray into Fitness

While Aryan's diet overhaul wasn't going as planned, he figured that maybe exercise could help. After all, every article he read about hair health mentioned the importance of "blood circulation" and "staying active." Plus, Aryan hadn't exactly been hitting the gym regularly or, let's be honest, at all. So, one Monday morning, Aryan decided to start a workout routine. Nothing too intense just a light jog around the neighborhood. He hadn't gone jogging since college, but how hard could it be? Aryan laced up his old running shoes, threw on some gym clothes, and headed out the door with the determination of a man who was convinced that this one jog might somehow stop his hair loss. He even put on one of those fitness trackers that counted his steps, calories, and (according to the marketing) probably had the ability to read his mind. The first few minutes weren't so bad. Aryan jogged at a leisurely pace, feeling pretty good about himself. "This isn't so hard," he thought. "I could totally do this every day." Then came minute six. By minute seven, Aryan was gasping for air. His legs felt like lead, his lungs were on fire, and his body was sending him very clear messages: *Why are we doing this? Stop immediately.* Aryan's leisurely jog turned into a desperate shuffle as he tried to make it back home without collapsing. When he finally stumbled through his front door, he collapsed on the couch, drenched in sweat and regretting every life choice that had led him to this moment. His fitness tracker beeped, proudly announcing that he had burned 87 calories.

"Eighty-seven calories?" Aryan groaned, throwing the tracker across the room. "That's, like, half a cookie."

Needless to say, Aryan's foray into fitness was short-lived. He briefly considered joining a gym, but after his disastrous jog, he decided that maybe he wasn't cut out for the whole "exercise" thing.

The Great Avocado Experiment

After his failure with spinach smoothies and jogging, Aryan was about ready to give up on the whole "healthy living" thing. But then, he read an article that changed everything. The article claimed that **avocados** yes, those trendy green fruits that millennials were obsessed with were a miracle food for hair health. They were full of healthy fats, vitamins, and other nutrients that supposedly did wonders for your hair, skin, and overall health. Aryan had never been much of an avocado guy, but he figured it was worth a shot. If avocados could somehow stop his hair from falling out, he was all in. So, the next time Aryan went grocery shopping, he loaded up on avocados. He didn't really know what to do with them, so he started with something simple: **avocado toast**. It was all over Instagram, and people swore by it, so it had to be good, right?

Aryan mashed up the avocado, spread it on a slice of toast, and took a bite. It was...surprisingly good.

"This is it," Aryan thought, chewing thoughtfully. "This is how I'm going to save my hair. Avocado toast every day."

For the next week, Aryan became an avocado-toast-making machine. Breakfast? Avocado toast. Lunch? Avocado toast with a side of eggs. Dinner? You guessed it avocado toast, with a sprinkle of chia seeds (because apparently, chia seeds were another miracle food). By the end of the week, Aryan's hair wasn't any thicker, but his Instagram feed was full of photos of perfectly plated avocado toast, and he had to admit, he felt pretty healthy. Still, deep down, Aryan knew that eating avocados wasn't going to magically fix his hairline. It might be good for him, sure, but there was no getting around the fact that genetics was doing most of the heavy lifting in his hair loss journey. But at least he could enjoy a good snack along the way.

Aryan's Encounter with Health Influencers: The Downward Spiral

As Aryan continued his quest to live a healthier life (for the sake of his hair, of course), he found himself falling deeper and deeper into the world of **health influencers**. You know the type people with perfect abs, glowing skin, and impossibly shiny hair who seemed to spend their entire lives drinking green juice and doing yoga on the beach. Aryan didn't really *want* to follow these people, but somehow, he found himself scrolling through their Instagram feeds late at night (once again an invitation to stress!!), wondering if maybe just maybe they knew something he didn't. One influencer, in particular, caught Aryan's attention. Her name was **Harmony**, and she was the epitome of wellness. Every post was perfectly curated morning yoga sessions, smoothie bowls that looked like works of art, and captions about "manifesting your best life." Harmony claimed that her daily routine of meditation, yoga, and plant-based eating for gut microbiome had transformed her life and her hair. Aryan was skeptical, but desperate times called for desperate measures. If Harmony's routine could make her hair look like that, maybe it could work for him too. Aryan decided to follow Harmony's advice, starting with her **morning routine**. According to her posts, she began each day with a glass of warm lemon water with honey, followed by a 45-minute yoga session and a green smoothie made with spinach, cucumber, and spirulina. Aryan wasn't sure what spirulina was, but he figured it couldn't be worse than the spinach banana smoothie disaster from earlier.

The next morning, Aryan tried to follow Harmony's routine. He made the lemon honey water (which tasted exactly like you'd expect sweet, sour and kind of pointless), struggled through a YouTube yoga class (in which he nearly pulled a muscle trying to do a downward dog), and then attempted to make the smoothie.

The result? A green, sludge-like substance that tasted like lawn clippings.

By the time Aryan finished gagging down the smoothie, he realized that Harmony's lifestyle was not for him. Inspite of the displeasure, Aryan tried the routine for few days. He didn't have the patience, the flexibility, or the taste buds for it. "Well, at least I tried," Finally one day Aryan muttered, pouring the rest of the smoothie down the drain. "Good luck, Harmony."

The Moment of Truth: Aryan's Lifestyle Epiphany

After weeks of failed smoothies, disastrous workouts, and a brief obsession with health influencers, Aryan came to a realization: **living a healthy lifestyle wasn't going to reverse his hair loss**. He had tried it all spinach, avocados, exercise, meditation and while some of it had made him feel healthier, none of it had made a dent in his hairline. But here's the thing: even though Aryan hadn't magically regrown his hair, he *did* feel better. He had more energy, his skin looked clearer, and he wasn't getting winded after climbing a flight of stairs. In a weird way, Aryan's quest to save his hair had turned into something bigger, it had forced him to take better care of himself, even if the results weren't what he had expected.

And maybe that was the real win.

Sure, Aryan's hair wasn't going to make a comeback, but at least he could look in the mirror and know that he was doing everything he could to stay healthy. And who knows? Maybe the avocado toast was doing something after all. If nothing else, it was a delicious way to start the day.

CHAPTER IV

"What Your Shampoo Won't Tell You"

If Aryan's quest to save his hair were a battle, then the **hair care industry** was the ultimate weapons dealer, armed with every product imaginable and ready to sell Aryan the dream of a full, luscious mane. Shampoos, conditioners, serums, hair masks Aryan had seen them all. And if the promises on the bottles were to be believed, these products could do everything short of bringing his hair back from the dead. But Aryan was a skeptic. He wasn't going to be fooled by fancy labels and smooth-talking ads, right?

Wrong.

As Aryan's hairline continued its slow retreat, he became more and more willing to believe that maybe just maybe there was a product out there that could save him. He wasn't ready to go bald, not yet. So, armed with his credit card and a renewed sense of hope, Aryan embarked on a journey through the confusing, overpriced, and often downright absurd world of hair care.

The Shampoo Aisle: Where Dreams (and Money) Go to Die

The shampoo aisle at Aryan's local grocery store was a battlefield of promises. Every bottle seemed to scream louder than the next, offering solutions to problems Aryan hadn't even realized he had.

"Volumize and strengthen thinning hair!"

"Boost growth with biotin and collagen!"

"Deep hydration for fuller, thicker locks!"

Aryan stood in front of the endless rows of brightly colored bottles, overwhelmed by choice. His current shampoo routine was embarrassingly simple he just grabbed whatever was on sale and smelled halfway decent. But clearly, that approach wasn't working anymore. His hair was thinning, and his current shampoo wasn't doing a damn thing to stop it. Aryan picked up a bottle that promised "instant thickness and maximum volume." He squinted at the label, trying to decipher the ingredients. *"Cocamidopropyl betaine panthenol hydrolyzed keratin."* Aryan's eyes glazed over. He didn't know what any of those words meant, but they sounded science-y, and science was good, right? Aryan threw the bottle in his cart, along with a conditioner that claimed to "strengthen hair from root to tip." As he wheeled his cart toward the checkout, Aryan felt a surge of optimism. "This is it," he thought. "This is the shampoo that's going to save my hair."

Spoiler alert: it wasn't.

Aryan's First Miracle Product: The Great Hair Serum Experiment

After few days of usage of the newly found shampoo friend, Like most people on a desperate quest to stop hair loss, Aryan quickly learned that shampoos alone weren't enough. No, the real magic was in **serums** or so the internet and social media told him. These magical little bottles of liquid promised to "stimulate hair growth," "reactivate dormant follicles," and even "reverse thinning in just two weeks." Aryan was intrigued. He hadn't realized his hair follicles were dormant, but if there was a serum that could wake them up, he was all in. After hours of scrolling through online reviews and before-and-after photos (most of which looked suspiciously Photoshopped), Aryan landed on a product that seemed promising: **Follicle bulb Fuel Pro Max**. The reviews were glowing. One guy claimed it had transformed his thinning hair into a "full, thick mane," while another swore that it had saved him from "certain baldness." Sure, it was expensive almost absurdly expensive but Aryan was desperate. He clicked "Buy Now" without hesitation. A few days later, the sleek black bottle arrived at his doorstep, packaged like it was some kind of luxury skincare product. The instructions were simple: after a head bath with a shampoo, apply a few drops to the scalp every night before bed and gently massage it in. Aryan did exactly that, carefully following the directions and half-expecting to wake up the next morning with a head full of thick, luxurious hair.

Of course, nothing happened.

But Aryan wasn't discouraged *yet*. Hair growth took time, after all. So, every night for the next three weeks, Aryan religiously took head bath with the shampoo, applied the serum, massaging his scalp like he was trying to coax his hair back to life. He even started imagining he could feel it working, tingling slightly under his fingers as if the follicles were slowly reawakening. But by the end of the two month, Aryan was forced to admit the truth: **Follicle bulb Fuel ProMax** wasn't the miracle product it had claimed to be. His hairline hadn't budged, his crown was still thinning, and the only thing Aryan had lost was a thousand bucks.

The DIY Disaster: When Aryan Took Hair Care into His Own Hands

After his serum experiment failed, Aryan briefly flirted with the idea of DIY hair treatments. The internet was full of them homemade hair masks, oils, even scalp scrubs that were supposed to stimulate growth. Aryan wasn't entirely convinced, but hey, if it worked for ancient civilizations, maybe it could work for him too. One popular DIY remedy kept popping up in Aryan's searches: **castor oil**. According to the wellness gurus of the world, castor oil was the ultimate hair saver. It could hydrate, strengthen, and even protect against hair loss. Some people even swore it could help hair grow faster. So, one evening, Aryan decided to give it a try. He warmed up a small bowl of castor oil, sat down in front of the bathroom mirror, and massaged the oil into his scalp. At first, it felt kind of nice warm and soothing, like he was at a spa (minus the relaxing part). But when Aryan woke up the next morning, things took a turn. His pillowcase was an oily mess, his hair felt like it had been dunked in a deep fryer, and worst of all, the castor oil *would* *not wash out*. Aryan spent nearly half an hour in the shower, scrubbing his hair furiously and muttering to himself, "How is this supposed to help?" Eventually, after multiple rounds of shampooing, Aryan emerged from the bathroom, his hair limp and greasy. The bathroom floor was full of hair which made Aryan even more anxious. The whole experience had been a disaster, and Aryan swore he'd never trust a DIY hair treatment again.

The Hair Mask Phase: When Aryan Got a Little Too Fancy

Despite his failures with serums and DIY treatments, Aryan wasn't ready to give up. He kept reading articles and watching YouTube tutorials, convinced that there was still a product out there that could help him. That's when he discovered **hair masks**. Apparently, hair masks were like deep-conditioning treatments that could "revitalize damaged hair" and "promote growth." Aryan wasn't sure how a hair mask could help his thinning hair, but if there was even a chance, he was willing to try it. He bought a jar of **revitalizing hair mask** from an overpriced salon and followed the instructions to a T. Apply generously to damp hair, leave on for 20 minutes, and rinse thoroughly. Now, Aryan had never done anything like this before, and sitting around his apartment with a towel wrapped around his head for 20 minutes made him feel ridiculous. He imagined his grandpa laughing from beyond the grave: *"What are you doing, son? It's just hair!"*

But Aryan powered through, determined to give the mask a fair shot.

After rinsing out the mask, Aryan stared at himself in the mirror, waiting for the miracle transformation. But all he saw was his same thinning hair, now slightly shinier and smelling faintly of lavender.

"Great," Aryan muttered. "At least my hair smells nice."

Aryan's Epiphany: The Hair-Care Marketing Trap

It wasn't until Aryan had spent months (and more money than he cared to admit) trying out every hair-care product under the sun that he finally had a moment of clarity. One night, as Aryan was slathering yet another expensive serum onto his scalp, he paused. *What am I doing?* he thought. *Is this really helping? Or am I just throwing money at a problem I can't fix?*The realization hit him like a ton of bricks. He had fallen into the **hair-care marketing trap** a never-ending cycle of buying products that promised miracles but delivered nothing more than a temporary placebo effect. The truth was, there was no shampoo, no serum, no miracle hair mask that was going to stop his genetic hair loss.

And that was a tough pill to swallow.

Aryan stared at the lineup of products on his bathroom shelf bottles and jars of every shape and size, each one claiming to be the solution to his thinning hair. He felt a little ridiculous, like he had been duped by the promises of glossy advertisements and influencer testimonials. But here's the thing: Aryan wasn't alone. **The hair-care**

industry thrives on selling hope in a bottle. Millions of people, just like Aryan, are out there desperately searching for a product that will fix their hair, when the truth is, sometimes hair loss just happens. And no amount of biotin-infused shampoo, serums, hair mask is going to change that.

The Simple Truth About Hair Care

After his epiphany, Aryan decided to strip things back to basics. He stopped obsessing over miracle products and focused on what really mattered: **simple, consistent hair care**. He found a gentle, sulfate-free shampoo that didn't promise the world but kept his hair clean and healthy. He used conditioner regularly to keep his hair soft, and once a week, he gave himself a relaxing scalp massage not because it was going to regrow his hair, but because it felt good. Aryan realized that sometimes, **less is more**. The more products he piled onto his scalp, the more overwhelmed he felt. But when he simplified his routine, he noticed something surprising: his hair didn't look worse. In fact, it looked...better. Maybe not thicker, but healthier.

Aryan's new mantra became, "Take care of what you have, and stop stressing about what you don't."

And you know what? It worked.

The Final Hair-Care Lesson: Keep It Simple

At the end of the day, Aryan's journey through the world of hair care taught him one valuable lesson: **there are no magic products**. No shampoo, conditioner, or serum is going to reverse years of genetics or stop hair loss in its tracks. But that doesn't mean you can't take care of the hair you've got. Aryan learned to appreciate the small things like a good scalp massage, a hydrating conditioner, and the joy of not having a sticky, greasy mess in his hair after trying out another ridiculous treatment.

And most importantly, Aryan learned to stop letting the promises on a shampoo bottle, serums and hair mask dictate how he felt about his hair.

CHAPTER V

"The Psychological Impact of hair "

Hair loss isn't just about losing hair it's about losing a part of your identity. For Aryan, it wasn't just a matter of looking in the mirror and seeing less hair. It was the emotional weight that came with it the creeping self-doubt, the awkward social moments, and the quiet, unshakable fear that maybe, just maybe, he wasn't the same person without his hair. Because here's the truth: when your hair starts thinning, so does your confidence. And as Aryan's hairline continued to recede, his self-assurance followed suit.

The Confidence Killer: Aryan's Growing Self-Consciousness

At first, Aryan didn't think much about his thinning hair. Sure, he noticed it, but he told himself it wasn't a big deal. *"It's just hair,"* he would say. *"Who cares?"* And for a while, that worked. But the more Aryan stared at his reflection, the more he started to notice the small changes. The way his hairline seemed to be inching backward, bit by bit. The way his once-thick hair was now looking a little sparse at the top. The way his forehead seemed to be getting more, well, *real estate*. It was subtle at first just a nagging thought at the back of his mind. But over time, that nagging thought grew louder. What had once been a passing glance in the mirror turned into a full-blown inspection. Aryan found himself spending way too much time analyzing his hair from every angle, tilting his head under the bathroom lights like he was some kind of follicle detective.

"Is it getting worse?" he would ask himself, squinting into the mirror. *"I swear it wasn't this bad last week.*

The more he fixated on his hair, the more self-conscious he became. And as his self-consciousness grew, so did his anxiety. Suddenly, Aryan wasn't just thinking about his hair in the bathroom. He was thinking about it at work, at the grocery store, on dates, and pretty much everywhere else. It was as if his hair loss had taken up permanent residence in his brain, quietly reminding him that his once-glorious hairline was slipping away.

The Cap Habit: Aryan's New Best Friend

As Aryan's self-consciousness grew, so did his reliance on **caps**. What had once been a casual accessory a cricket cap here, a beanie there became a full-blown security blanket. Aryan started wearing caps all the time. And I mean *all* the time. It started innocently enough. A cap on a lazy weekend, maybe when he was running errands or meeting friends for brunch. But soon, the cap habit spiraled. Aryan wouldn't leave the house without one. Going to the grocery store? Cap. Grabbing coffee with Pooja? Cap. Meeting friends for a casual dinner? You bet there was a cap involved. The thing about caps is that they hide everything. Under a cap, Aryan could pretend his hair was fine. The thinning spots were out of sight, and as far as he was concerned, they were out of mind too. Caps became his way of *controlling* the situation. If people couldn't see his hair, they couldn't judge it, right?

Of course, Aryan's friends started to notice. Umesh , being Umesh, had no filter when it came to pointing out Aryan's cap obsession.

"Dude, why are you always wearing a cap now?" Umesh asked one night, sipping his beer and eyeing Aryan's cap. "You hiding something under there?"

Aryan shrugged, playing it off. "Just like caps," he muttered, taking a swig of his drink.

But Umesh wasn't buying it. "Yeah, well, you're starting to look like one of those guys who wears a cap indoors. You know the *cool dad* type."

Aryan rolled his eyes, but inside, he felt a pang of anxiety. He knew Umesh wasn't wrong. He *was* hiding something. But the idea of taking off his cap? That was terrifying. What if people noticed his thinning hair? What if they whispered about it behind his back? What if... they judged him?

The Dating Disasters: Aryan's Hairline Anxiety in Love

Hair loss doesn't just mess with your day-to-day life it also screws with your dating game. And for Aryan, the stress of dating with a receding hairline was next-level anxiety. One of the worst moments came during a date with a girl named Aditi. They'd met online, exchanged a few flirty messages, and agreed to meet for drinks. Aryan liked Aditi, she was funny, smart, and had a great smile. He should have been excited about the date. But instead, Aryan was fixated on one thing: his hair.

The date started off fine good conversation, a few laughs but then, somewhere between drinks and appetizers, Aditi casually asked, "So, you're a cap guy, huh?"

Aryan froze. The question was innocent enough, but to him, it felt like a direct attack on his hairline. "Uh, yeah," Aryan stammered, forcing a laugh. "I like caps."

Aditi smiled, but Aryan couldn't shake the feeling that she was secretly wondering what was *under* the cap. Did she think he was bald? Was she waiting for him to take it off and reveal the truth? The rest of the date was a blur of awkward moments as Aryan's anxiety spiraled out of control. By the time they said goodnight, Aryan was convinced that his hair or lack thereof was all Aditi could think about.

Needless to say, there was no second date.

The Candid Photo Disaster: Aryan's Social Media Nightmare

But the worst moment the one that sent Aryan into a full-blown hair crisis came during Umesh's birthday party. It was a fun night. Aryan had actually forgotten about his hair for a while, enjoying drinks and laughs with friends. He was even starting to feel like his old self again. That is, until the next morning, when Umesh posted a series of photos from the party on Facebook and Instagram. One of the photos caught Aryan off guard. It was a candid shot, taken from slightly above, and it showed the back of Aryan's head. More specifically, it showed the **thinning crown** of Aryan's head in all its glory. Aryan stared at the photo in horror.

Was it really that bad? His mind started racing. *Had everyone seen it? Had they all noticed?* Aryan felt his stomach drop as he imagined all his friends scrolling through Facebook and Instagram, looking at the photo and thinking, *Wow, Aryan's really losing his hair.*

The comments under the photo were innocent people tagging each other, reminiscing about the party but to Aryan, it felt like everyone was silently judging his hairline. He considered untagging himself, or better yet, asking Umesh to take the photo down altogether. But what would that look like? Wouldn't it be even *more* obvious?

Instead, Aryan did what any rational person would do: he threw on a cap, closed his laptop, and spent the rest of the day sulking in front of the TV.

The Turning Point: Aryan's Hairline Epiphany

It wasn't until a few weeks after the Facebook and Instagram photo disaster that Aryan finally had an epiphany. He'd spent so much time and energy worrying about his hair hiding it, stressing about it, obsessing over it that he'd forgotten something important: **It's just hair.**

Sure, hair is important. It's tied to our identity, our confidence, our sense of self. But at the end of the day, it's just one part of who we are. And the truth was, Aryan was tired. He was tired of hiding behind caps, tired of avoiding candid photos, tired of letting his hair (or lack thereof) dictate how he felt about himself.

So, one morning, Aryan made a decision. He stood in front of the bathroom mirror, took off his cap, and stared at his reflection. His hairline wasn't what it used to be. His crown was thinning. But he was still Aryan. The same Aryan who made people laugh, who had great friends, who was capable of so much more than obsessing over his hair. And in that moment, Aryan let go. He wasn't going to let his hair or the loss of it control his life anymore. He wasn't going to hide behind caps, avoid photos, or worry about what people thought. He was going to own it. And if that meant rocking a receding hairline or thinning crown, so be it.

Aryan's Journey to Acceptance: Rebuilding Confidence

The funny thing about letting go of something is that, once you do, it loses its power over you. After Aryan decided to stop stressing about his hair, he noticed something amazing: he started to feel more confident.

It wasn't an overnight transformation Aryan still had moments of insecurity, and he still wore caps sometimes (mostly because he liked them, not because he *needed* them). But slowly, Aryan started to care less about what other people thought of his hair. He stopped analyzing his reflection every morning, stopped avoiding social situations where his thinning hair might be on display, and most importantly, stopped letting his hair define his self-worth. And here's the kicker: the less Aryan stressed about his hair, the better he felt. He realized that confidence wasn't about having a perfect head of hair it was about how you carried yourself, how you showed up in the world, how you treated the people around you. Aryan's hair might have been thinning, but his confidence was growing.

The Psychological Lesson: Hair Loss Isn't the End

At the end of the day, Aryan's journey through hair loss wasn't just about losing hair. It was about learning to accept himself thinning hairline and all. It was about letting go of the idea that his worth was tied to his appearance, and realizing that who he was as a person mattered far more than the number of hairs on his head. For Aryan, the psychological impact of hair loss had been real. It had made him feel insecure, anxious, and self-conscious in ways he never expected. But by the end of it, he'd come out the other side stronger, more confident, and with a new perspective on life and hair. Because here's the truth: hair loss might change the way you look, but it doesn't change who you are. And once Aryan figured that out, he realized he was free. Free to be himself, free to live his life, and free to rock his thinning hairline with confidence.

CHAPTER VI

"Maintenance of Long-Lasting Healthy Hair"

By the time Aryan reached his 30s, he had been through the emotional wringer of hair loss. He'd battled genetics, lost sleep over stress-induced shedding, and thrown money at every miracle hair product under the sun. He'd spiraled into the depths of self-doubt, stared too long at candid photos of his thinning hair, and even briefly considered moving to a tropical island where everyone wore hats all the time.

But then, something changed.

Aryan stopped chasing miracle cures and started focusing on something much simpler: **taking care of himself**. No more gimmicks, no more late-night Googling for "instant hair regrowth," and no more DIY hair masks that made his apartment smell like an oil spill. Instead, Aryan decided to focus on what he *could* control his overall health, his habits, and his attitude.

And as it turned out, those small, consistent changes made a bigger difference than any bottle of serum ever could.

The Morning Walk:
Aryan's Simple Secret to Feeling Good

It all started with a **45 min morning walk**. Neha, his friend who was always full of unsolicited (but often good) advice, had been telling him for months that getting some fresh air, and exercise first thing in the morning was the key to feeling better both mentally and physically. Aryan had always brushed it off. He wasn't a "morning person," and the thought of waking up early to walk around the block sounded like pure torture.

But one day, after another frustrating week of watching his hairline inch backward, Aryan decided to give it a try. What did he have to lose, besides a few more strands of hair?

So, one bright, crisp morning, Aryan dragged himself out of bed, threw on some sneakers, and headed out the door for a walk. The first few minutes were rough his body wasn't used to moving before 9 a.m., and the chilly air made him wonder if this was all a mistake. But as he kept walking, something surprising happened. He started to feel... **Good**.

The fresh air cleared his head, and the movement woke up his body in a way that felt energizing rather than exhausting. By the time he returned home, Aryan felt refreshed and surprisingly alert like he'd already conquered part of the day before it even really started.

He decided to do it again the next day. And the next. Soon, the morning walk became part of his daily routine, and Aryan noticed something strange: he was feeling better not just physically, but mentally. The walk gave him a chance to clear his mind, get his blood and energy flowing. These small steps helped him start the day on the right foot (pun intended). Plus, according to every health blog out there, good circulation was key to maintaining healthy hair, so he figured the walk, was probably helping his scalp too.

Whether it was the fresh air or the boost in circulation, Aryan didn't know, but his hair seemed to appreciate the new routine too. The constant shedding slowed down, and while his hairline wasn't exactly surging forward, it wasn't retreating as fast anymore either.

Aryan's Foray Into Yoga: Less Stress, More Hair?

After mastering the morning walk, Aryan decided to tackle something else Neha had been bugging him about: **yoga**.

Now, Aryan had tried yoga before, and it hadn't gone well. His first attempt had left him sore, sweaty, and more stressed out than before. But Neha swore by it, and she insisted that yoga wasn't just about stretching it was about **reducing stress**. And as Aryan had learned the hard way, **stress and hair loss were best friends**. The more stressed Aryan got, the more hair he seemed to lose.

So, one Saturday morning, Aryan signed up for a beginner's yoga class at the local studio with Pallavi. He walked in feeling a little apprehensive, but determined to give it another shot.

This time the class started slow, with some simple breathing exercises and gentle stretches. Aryan was still skeptical how was breathing supposed to help his hairline? But as the class went on, he found himself relaxing. The instructor's soothing voice guided him through poses that were surprisingly manageable, and by the end of the class, Aryan felt... calm. Like, *actually calm*. Aryan continued doing yoga for the next few weeks. He did yoga aasana like Sirsasana, Sarvangasana, Adho Mukha Svanasana, Uttasana, Vajrasana, Balasana, Matyasana, Pavanmukhtasana. Also Aryan learned doing pranayama like *Anulom Vilom, Kapalbhati, Bhramari, Ujjayi*. Aryan really felt calm and serene after performing these yoga. He wasn't sure if yoga was doing anything for his hair, but it was definitely doing something for his stress levels. And since stress was a known hair killer, Aryan figured less stress could only be a good thing. But in reality it was the yoga which helped him reduce stress, increase blood flow to his scalp and hair and thereby reduce hair loss.

"The Zen of Aryan: A Meditation Adventure"

Aryan had never been the kind of guy who could sit still. In fact, the idea of just sitting like, literally *sitting still*, doing nothing seemed like a complete waste of time. His mind was always buzzing, moving from one thought to the next faster than he could keep up. And if he had a free moment, well, why would he spend it sitting on a cushion with his eyes closed when there were a million other things he could be doing?

But as he started his journey of self-improvement with morning walk and yoga, Aryan kept stumbling upon one word that seemed to pop up everywhere: **meditation**. On the podcasts he listened to, in the self-care articles he read, Brahmakumaris follower sister Shivani preachings, even from friends who swore it had "changed their lives." And at first, Aryan didn't buy it. He couldn't understand how doing *nothing* could somehow make you feel like *everything*. But then, there was Neha. Neha, her walking, yoga-practicing, avocado-loving friend, who never missed an opportunity to tell Aryan about the "power of mindfulness" and how meditation could help with his stress, his hair loss, and basically all of life's problems. She made it sound so simple just close your eyes, focus on your breath, visualize and boom, instant zen.

Aryan wasn't convinced, but he had to admit, Neha had a point. Stress was a big part of his hair-loss journey, and he'd tried just about everything else so why not give meditation a shot?

Aryan's First (Failed) Attempt at Meditation

One morning , after his usual morning walk, Aryan decided to give this whole meditation thing a try once again. He found a video on YouTube titled **"10-Minute Guided Meditation for Beginners"** and clicked play. The voice on the video was soft and soothing, like the woman was speaking from a cloud, which made Aryan feel slightly ridiculous.

"Find a comfortable seated position," the voice said. "Close your eyes, and take a deep breath in... and out."

Aryan shifted around on his couch, trying to find that "comfortable" position. His leg was falling asleep, his back wasn't quite straight, and he couldn't figure out what to do with his hands. But he gave it a shot, closing his eyes and taking a deep breath.

"Now, bring your focus to your breath," the voice continued. "Feel the sensation of the air as it enters your nose, and as it leaves your mouth."

Aryan inhaled, trying to focus on his breath. *In through the nose, out through the mouth.* Simple enough. But just as he was getting into it, his mind started to wander. *Did I remember to pay that bill? Did I leave the gas in kitchen on? What's that weird sound coming from the fridge?*

"Gently let go of any thoughts that arise," the voice said, as if reading his mind. "And return to the breath."

Aryan tried, he really did. But his thoughts just kept coming. *Is this working? Am I doing it right? Is this supposed to feel relaxing? Because all I feel is anxious.*

The ten minutes felt like an eternity. By the time the video ended, Aryan wasn't feeling zen, he was feeling exhausted. "Well, that was pointless," he muttered, hitting pause and shoving his phone aside. He didn't feel any less stressed. If anything, he felt *more* stressed. How were you supposed to stop your thoughts from running wild when that was basically all your brain did?

The (Slightly Better) Second Attempt

But Aryan wasn't ready to give up just yet this time. He figured maybe the problem wasn't meditation itself maybe it was just *him.* Maybe he was thinking about it the wrong way. So, the next morning, he tried again.

This time, he decided to keep it simple. No guided videos, no calming background music. Just him, his breath, and five minutes of silence. He sat down on his bedroom floor, crossed his legs, and closed his eyes.

And then, he did nothing.

At first, his brain was all over the place, jumping from one thought to another like a ping-pong ball. *What should I have for lunch today? Is it going to rain? Why did I say that stupid thing at work yesterday?* But Aryan tried not to fight it. He remembered something Neha had said: "The point of meditation isn't to *empty* your mind it's to just be *aware* of your thoughts."

So, Aryan let the thoughts come. He noticed them, acknowledged them, and tried to let them pass. And slowly, very slowly, he felt his body start to relax. He noticed the rhythm of his breath, the rise and fall of his chest, the way the air felt as it entered and left his nose. And for just a moment a brief, fleeting moment Aryan felt a little bit of peace. Sure, his mind still wandered, and sure, he still didn't feel like he was getting it "right," but when he opened his eyes five minutes later, something was different. He felt calmer. Lighter. Like he'd just taken a break from all the noise in his head.

Maybe, just maybe, there was something to this meditation thing after all.

Finding His Groove: Aryan's Meditation Routine

Over the next few weeks, Aryan made meditation a part of his daily routine. It wasn't always easy in fact, some days, it was downright impossible to sit still and focus on his breath. But the more he practiced, the more he found himself looking forward to those quiet moments. It became a chance to check in with himself, to press pause on all the craziness of life, and to just... *be.*

And the results? They were subtle at first. Aryan noticed he wasn't as quick to get frustrated at little things like when someone cut him off in traffic, or when his computer froze right in the middle of a Zoom meeting. He felt a little more patient, a little more grounded. And on those days when his hair loss felt like a punch to the gut, meditation gave him the tools to handle it to breathe through the panic, let go of the anxiety, and remind himself that he was more than his hairline.

Over time, those five minutes of meditation turned into ten. And then fifteen. Sometimes, Aryan would light a candle or play some soft music in the background. Other times, he'd just sit on his couch, close his eyes, and breathe. It didn't matter how he did it what mattered was that he showed up for himself. That he gave himself permission to stop, to rest, to reconnect with the simple, beautiful act of breathing.

Aryan's Meditation Epiphany

One morning Aryan sat down to meditate as usual. His mind was buzzing, thoughts racing from one worry to the next since yesterday. But instead of fighting it, Aryan let it all go. He took a deep breath, closed his eyes, and sat with whatever came up. And in that stillness, something clicked. It wasn't just about sitting still or breathing deeply. Meditation was about **acceptance**. Accepting the chaos, the stress, the uncertainty of life and finding peace in the middle of it all. It was about learning to sit with his thoughts, even when they were messy, even when they were uncomfortable, and realizing that they didn't have to control him. And in that moment, Aryan realized something big: his hair loss wasn't something he had to fight against or run away from. It was just another part of his journey one that he could navigate with grace, with calm, and with confidence. Meditation hadn't just helped him find peace with his hair it had helped him find peace with *himself*.

The Everyday Magic of Meditation

From that day on, meditation wasn't just a practice it was a part of who Aryan was. A way to find stillness in the chaos, a way to connect to something deeper than the stress of work, hair, and all the everyday challenges life threw his way. He didn't need to be perfect at it (and trust me, he wasn't). He didn't need to empty his mind or reach some kind of enlightenment. All he needed to do was show up, breathe, and be present. And in that presence, Aryan found something he'd been missing for a long time: **peace of mind**. It wasn't a direct cure for hair loss, and it didn't magically solve all his problems too. But it gave him the strength to handle them to see things clearly, to let go of what he couldn't control, and to focus on what he could. And this attitude helped him control his hair loss and solve his problems.

Stress = External pressure / Coping ability.

Meditation helped Aryan increase his coping ability to face all the external pressures of his life. As a results with increased coping ability, his stress levels reduced drastically and so his hair loss and hair thinning.

So, every morning, after his walk and before his day really began, Aryan sat down, closed his eyes, and just... breathed. And in those moments of stillness, he found a calm that no shampoo, no serum, and no hair mask could ever provide.

And that? That was the real magic.

The magical elixir triad of healthy mind, body and hair

Finally after many failed attempts, Aryan discovered **the triad of early morning 45 mins of nature walk, yoga and meditation is the magical elixir for healthy mind, healthy body and hence healthy hair**. Aryan could feel his mind getting stable, body getting healthier and see his hairs getting thicker and darker . And now it was the time to focus on yet another important aspect of health. It was the most ignored component in Aryan's life. The diet.

Aryan Bites Back - A Hair-Raising Diet

Aryan our IT hero, the guy who can debug code faster than you can say "network error," but who's losing hair faster than you can say "404 Not Found." Aryan tried everything to fix his thinning hair, special shampoos, bizarre online mask and DIY formulations, the smoothies that promised to give him a full head of hair overnight (spoiler alert: it didn't). But one thing Aryan hadn't really considered was… his diet.

Of course, no lifestyle overhaul would be complete without addressing **diet**. Aryan had never been one to pay much attention to what he ate. As long as it tasted good and didn't require too much effort to make, it was fair game. Pizza, burgers, frozen dinners Aryan's kitchen looked like the after-party of a late-night college study session.

But the more Aryan read about hair health, the more he realized that diet played a huge role in how your hair looked and felt. If he wanted to keep what hair he had left, to make the hairs thicker, he needed to start feeding his body and his follicles something a little more nutritious. The idea of giving up his favorite fast foods made Aryan sad, but he didn't want to go bald either, so he decided to make some changes.

Aryan's first stop was Google obviously. And one thing became very clear to him: **protein, vitamins, minerals pro and prebiotics** were crucial. Feed your gut to grow more hair. Aryan realized that hair is made mostly of a protein called keratin, which acts like the code for strong, healthy strands. Aryan's diet, consisting mostly of instant noodlcs, pizza, and soda, wasn't cutting it. The man needed protein. He swapped out the chips for **nuts and seeds**, loaded with protein and omega-3 fatty acids, which are like the magical coding wizards for hair strength. Almonds, walnuts, chia seeds you name it, Aryan was crunching on it.

Instead of pizza for lunch every day, he started adding soybeans, sprouts and eggsto his meals. Protein in eggs helped him boost his biotin intake (goodbye, weak hair), and soybeans and sprouts gave his follicles the strength they needed to hold on for dear life. And for vegetarian days (because Aryan was a modern, balanced kind of guy), he'd turn to **lentils, beans, and chickpeas**. They were his plant-based powerhouses, great for protein and even better for his thinning hairline.

Aryan realized that vitamins were like the software patches his hair needed to run smoothly. It was time for an upgrade, and he wasn't going to skimp on the essentials.

Vitamin A: The Scalp Conditioner

Vitamin A helps produce sebum, the natural oil that conditions your scalp. It's like built-in hair care! Aryan started munching on **sweet potatoes, carrots, and leafy greens**. A carrot a day? More like a better hair day!

Vitamin B-Complex: The Stress Reliever

Aryan loved his stress (who doesn't when you work in IT?), but his hair didn't. B vitamins, like **B7 (biotin)**, act like a calming interface between stress and hair loss. So Aryan started adding **whole grains, avocados, and bananas** to his breakfasts. And let's face it, avocado toast just makes you look cooler at the office.

Vitamin C: The Hair Shield

Vitamin C is an antioxidant superhero, protecting hair from free radicals (bad guys) and boosting collagen production (the good stuff). So Aryan found himself eating **oranges, berries, and bell peppers** as if they were the snacks of the gods.

Vitamin D: Sunshine in a Bowl

Aryan did start the morning walk since a while, But he learned that Vitamin D is crucial for hair follicle health. He began having **mushrooms**, and even a fortified bowl of cereal to his diet. Suddenly, Aryan was feeling sunny, inside and out.

Vitamin E: The Blood Circulation Pro

Vitamin E improves blood circulation, which means better nutrient delivery to the scalp. For that, Aryan loaded up on **spinach, nuts, and sunflower seeds**. A little green in your diet can go a long way, and Aryan was on a roll.

Minerals: The Anti-Hair Loss Firefighters

Just like any good system needs constant monitoring, Aryan's hair needed minerals to keep it from crashing. Iron, zinc, and magnesium were his hair's first responders.

Iron: The Hair's Uber Driver

Iron delivers oxygen to the cells, including those hardworking hair follicles. Without it, hair can be dry, dull, and fall out. Aryan added **lentils and dark leafy greens** to his plate. Pretty soon, he felt like his hair had its very own chauffeur service.

Zinc: The Hair Repair Specialist

Zinc helps with tissue growth and repair. It's like having a helpdesk for your hair. Aryan started popping **pumpkin seeds** and adding more **beans** to his soups and salads. He even discovered how much he loved **oysters**, which are zinc-packed. A hair-reviving delicacy!

Magnesium: The Stress Buster

Magnesium reduces stress, and you already know what stress does to hair (spoiler: it makes it jump ship). Aryan picked up **bananas, avacados andleafy greens** for his magnesium needs.

Gut Health: The Hair-Happy Microbiome

It turns out that gut health is crucial for nutrient absorption, and a healthy gut equals happy hair. Aryan had a eureka moment when he found out about prebiotics and probiotics. It was like discovering a hidden code that made everything work better.

Prebiotic Foods

Aryan started including **garlic, onions, and asparagus** in his meals. These foods feed the good bacteria in the gut, which, in turn, helps nutrient absorption.

Probiotic Foods

For the probiotics, Aryan loaded up on **yogurt, buttermilk, sauerkraut, and kefir**. Think of them as the friendly bacteria that keep your gut happy and your hair follicles dancing.

Hydration: The Essential Coolant

Aryan didn't want to be the guy who passed out from dehydration during a code freeze, so he upped his water intake. At least 8-10 glasses a day. And if plain water was too "meh," he threw in some lemon or cucumber slices to make it more refreshing. A hydrated body meant a hydrated scalp, and that's just good for everyone involved.

Aryan's new diet wasn't exactly revolutionary or fancy, he wasn't going full vegan or anything but he was making small, manageable changes that felt sustainable. He still indulged in pizza from time to time, but he balanced it out with healthier choices. And while it wasn't a miracle cure, Aryan noticed that his hair felt stronger, shinier, and, dare we say, happier? It wasn't a full-on lion's mane, but he could run his fingers through it without seeing a mini blizzard of hair fall out.

Hair Care Routine: Keeping It Simple

Now that Aryan had a handle on his diet and exercise routine, it was time to tackle his **hair care routine**. After months of experimenting with every product imaginable, Aryan had finally accepted that there was no magic shampoo or serum that was going to reverse his hair loss.

But that didn't mean he couldn't take care of the hair he had left.

Aryan stripped his routine back to basics. He found a gentle, sulfate-free shampoo that didn't strip his hair of its natural oils, and a hydrating conditioner that kept his hair soft and manageable. No more "miracle" products, no more serums that smelled like exotic flowers but did nothing to help his hair. Just simple, consistent care.

Once a week, Aryan gave himself a **scalp massage**. It wasn't fancy just a few minutes of gently massaging his scalp to stimulate blood flow. He'd read somewhere that scalp massages could help keep the follicles healthy, and even if that wasn't true, it felt good. And after everything Aryan had been through with his hair, he figured he deserved a little pampering.

His new routine wasn't revolutionary, but it worked. His hair was growing back in thickness to some extent, luscious waves, and was healthier. It felt stronger, and the constant shedding had stopped. However he couldn't get back his receding hairline back to his original once. And for Aryan, that was enough.

The Slow, Steady Results: Aryan's New Outlook on Hair (and Life)

After a few months of sticking to his new routine **morning walks, yoga, meditation, a better diet, and a simple hair-care regimen** Aryan started to notice some real changes. His hair wasn't miraculously growing back, but it looked better. Healthier. Stronger. The thinning had slowed, and while his hairline wasn't moving forward, it wasn't retreating as fast anymore either.

But more importantly, Aryan *felt* better. His energy levels were higher, his stress was lower, and he had regained a sense of control over his body (and his hair). He wasn't chasing miracle cures or obsessing over every lost strand anymore. He was taking care of himself from the inside out.

And here's the thing: it wasn't just about his hair. Aryan realized that this journey had been about so much more than trying to hold onto his hairline. It had been about learning to take care of himself in a way that felt sustainable, balanced, and dare he say it enjoyable.

Sure, Aryan still had days where he wished his hairline would magically spring back to where it was in his 20s. But he no longer let those thoughts control him. He was more than his hair. He was healthier, happier, and more confident than he had been in years.

Aryan's Final Takeaway: Balance is Key

At the end of the day, Aryan's journey to healthier hair was really a journey to a **healthier life**. He'd learned that taking care of yourself whether it's your hair, your body, or your mind isn't about doing one big thing or finding a miracle cure. It's about **the small, consistent actions you take every day**. It's about finding balance between treating yourself and taking care of yourself, between indulgence and discipline, between doing what you love and doing what's good for you.

Aryan might not have regained his full head of hair, but he'd regained something more important: his confidence, his health, and a new perspective on life. But then life has so much of surprises. One such surprise was waiting to be unfolded in next few days which Aryan must not have ever thought.

CHAPTER VII

"The Follicular Reunion"

Aryan wasn't expecting much from the high school reunion. In fact, he had actively avoided it for weeks, hovering over the "Maybe" RSVP on Facebook like he was weighing whether to walk into a lion's den. Reunions, after all, were social minefields especially when you were dealing with hair loss. Who wanted to sit around while people you hadn't seen in years threw out backhanded compliments like, "Wow, you look so different!" or, even worse, "You still look the same!" (*translation: bald*).

But Umesh, being Umesh, had worn him down with endless texts and guilt trips about "friendship" and "not bailing." So there Aryan was, driving toward the old high school gymnasium, sweating through his shirt, hoping the dim lighting would be forgiving to his hairline which had receded. As he parked his car and glanced at himself in the rearview mirror, Aryan mentally brace himself for a night of awkward small talk and forced nostalgia. What he didn't expect was that this night would mark the beginning of his *hair resurrection*.

The Surprise Encounter

The gym was filled with familiar faces well, mostly familiar. It was like looking at a blurry photograph where everyone was vaguely recognizable, but just a little off. Some people had filled out, others had slimmed down, and more than a few had fully embraced the "dad bod" lifestyle.

Aryan mingled, sipping a beer and nodding along as Umesh regaled their classmates with exaggerated tales of their high school pranks. Even though Aryan had started yoga and meditation for mental peace with hair, his mind wasn't fully in it he was distracted by the occasional glances at his own reflection in the mirrors lining the gym. His hairline was a constant source of anxiety, even here. What would people think? Did they notice? Were they silently comparing the "then" and "now" of his hair?

Just as he was about to slink away to the bathroom for a quick hair check, a voice called out from across the room, "Aryan? Is that you?"

Aryan turned, and his jaw nearly hit the floor. Walking toward him was **Mayur** his old high school buddy, the guy who had gone bald in his early 20s. Except, something was different. No, *everything* was different. Mayur wasn't bald anymore. In fact, he had a full, thick head of hair, complete with the kind of sharp, defined hairline that Aryan had long since given up on.

"Mayur?!" Aryan stammered, blinking in disbelief as his friend came closer.

Mayur laughed. "Yeah, man! Been a while, huh?"

Aryan shook his head, still trying to process what he was seeing. "Dude, you... you've got hair!"

Mayur grinned and ran a hand through his thick, perfectly styled mane. "I know. Pretty crazy, right?"

Crazy was an understatement. The last time Aryan had seen Mayur, he had been fully bald embracing the smooth, shiny look like a champion. But now? Now Mayur looked like he had stepped out of a hair product commercial.

"Okay, seriously," Aryan said, his eyes wide, "what's going on? The last time I saw you, you were bald. Like, *bald* bald."

Mayur chuckled, clearly enjoying Aryan's reaction. "Yeah, I was. For a long time. But I decided to do something about it."

Aryan leaned in, intrigued. "What do you mean? Hair plugs? A wig? What's your secret?"

Mayur shook his head. "Nope. None of that. I got a **hair transplant**."

Aryan blinked. "A hair transplant? Like, for real?"

"Yup," Mayur said, nodding. "It's not what you think, though. It's not like those horror stories you hear from the '90s with plugs and weird, patchy results. This is the real deal *follicular unit extraction*, or FUE for short. Basically, they take healthy hair follicles from the back of your head, where the hair is still thick, and they transplant them to the areas where you're thinning or bald. It's your own hair, so it looks totally natural. And it stays!"

Aryan was floored. He had heard about hair transplants, but in his mind, they were still risky and outdated, the kind of thing only celebrities with too much money would try. But Mayur? Mayur was living proof that it worked and worked well.

"Dude, I had no idea it was even possible to get results like that," Aryan said, still staring at Mayur's hair in awe. "I mean, look at you! You're basically *the old you* again."

Mayur laughed. "Yeah, it feels good, man. Honestly, I was bald for so long, I didn't think I'd care about having hair again. But once I started looking into it and saw how far the technology had come, I figured, why not? Best decision I ever made."

"Was it, like, super expensive?" Aryan asked, already imagining Rupees sign dancing in front of his eyes.

"It wasn't cheap," Mayur admitted, "but it's a lot more affordable now than it used to be. Plus, I found a really good doctor, and he worked with me to figure out a plan. Honestly, it's worth every penny. I wake up every morning, look in the mirror, and see my old hairline. It's like I hit rewind on my hair."

Aryan couldn't stop thinking about it. The idea that there was a way to get his hairline back *his real hair line* seemed too good to be true. And yet, Mayur was standing right in front of him, living proof that it was possible.

For the rest of the night, Aryan's mind was spinning. He couldn't stop staring at Mayur's hair and imagining what it would be like to have his own hairline back. The more he thought about it, the more the idea of a hair transplant started to take root in his brain.

Could this be the answer? Could he really get his lost hair back?

With yoga, meditation , morning walk and diet, Aryan had managed to stopped the hair shedding and made his existing hairs thicker and darker. But now after meeting Mayur, a new optimism arose in Aryan's mind. He wanted to regain the glory of 20's once again. He wanted his lost hair line back. And yes, the answer was hairtransplant.

As Aryan drove home from the reunion, he couldn't stop replaying Mayur's words in his head: *"It's worth every penny."* The idea of a hair transplant seemed almost too good to be true, but the evidence was staring him in the face. Mayur wasn't just pulling off the look he was thriving. Confident, happy, and completely at ease with his appearance. That was something Aryan hadn't felt in a long time.

By the time Aryan got home, he had made up his mind. He was going to look into it. He was going to see if this whole hair transplant thing could work for him.

The Hair Transplant Saga

A few days later, Aryan found himself sitting in the waiting room of a hair restoration clinic, flipping nervously through a magazine and trying to ignore the butterflies in his stomach. He had done his research, read the reviews, and even watched a few YouTube videos of people documenting their hair transplant journeys. It all looked promising. But still, the idea of undergoing a procedure to move hair from one part of his head to another? It felt surreal.

Finally, the nurse called his name, and Aryan was ushered into a consultation room. He was greeted by **Dr. Mishra**, a friendly, young man with the kind of confidence in his body language and the consultation began for his hair transplant. At the end of consultation, Aryan was super excited and ready for the procedure. Aryan fixed up a date for his procedure immediately and went back home filled with excitement.

Finally the day of procedure arrived and Aryan came to the clinic for his hair-transplant. The procedure itself was surprisingly smooth. Aryan had expected more pain, but aside from a few initial pinches from the local anesthesia, it was mostly painless. **Dr. Mishra** and his team worked methodically, extracting hair follicles from the back of Aryan's head and carefully transplanting them to the thinning areas along his hairline.

The whole process just took few hours, but by the end of it, Aryan felt a strange sense of calm. It wasn't just about getting his hair back it was about taking control of something he had felt powerless over for years.

But in that moment, Aryan saw something he hadn't seen in a long time: **hope**.

Over the next few months, Aryan's hair began to grow. The hairline that had once been in full retreat was now advancing, cm by cm, toward its original position. The thickening hair, the sharper hairline it was all coming back to his 20's, and with it, so was his confidence. A year after the transplant, Aryan stood in front of the mirror, running his fingers through his full head of hair. He looked good. He felt good. And for the first time in a long time, he was thinking about his hairline in a very positive way. His hair was back, and with it came a sense of completion.

Aryan's Hair Journey Comes Full Circle

As Aryan sat down with Mayur for a drink a year after the reunion, he couldn't stop smiling. Mayur, noticing the grin, raised an eyebrow. "What's up, man?"

Aryan chuckled and ran a hand through his hair, still marveling at the fullness. "I just can't believe it. I mean, look at me. I have my hairline again. It feels like a dream."

Mayur clinked his glass against Aryan's. "Told you it was worth it."

And as Aryan sipped his drink, feeling the weight of his once-dominant hair anxiety lift, he realized that, yeah it really *was* worth it. Not just for the hair, but for the confidence, the self-assurance, and the sense that he had finally reclaimed a part of himself that he thought was gone forever.

For Aryan, the journey wasn't just about getting his hair back. It was about finding peace with himself whether he had hair or not. The transplant? That was just the icing on the cake.

And life, as far as Aryan was concerned, felt pretty damn complete.

Conclusion: The Hairline That Stayed In Place

If you had asked Aryan one and half year ago how he felt about his hair, he would've laughed nervously, adjusted his cap, and quickly changed the subject. Hair loss was a terrifying reality, the kind that lurked in the shadows like a bad horror movie villain, slowly creeping toward him with a pair of invisible scissors.

But here's the thing about hair loss that Aryan didn't realize at the time: it's not the end of the world. In fact, it's not even the end of your hair. Sure, Aryan's hairline had decided to make a gradual retreat, and yes, there were a few thinning spots he could no longer ignore. But as Aryan learned, hair loss wasn't the tragedy he'd once imagined it to be. It was just... part of life. A slightly inconvenient, mildly frustrating, but totally manageable part of life.

Because, as Aryan now knew, it's not the hair on your head that defines you it's the way you handle losing it. And Aryan? Well, after all the stress, the failed products, the emotional ups and downs, and the lifestyle changes, Aryan had come out the other side stronger, healthier, and surprisingly, a lot more confident.

The Great Hair Epiphany: It's Just Hair

The biggest lesson Aryan learned on his hair loss journey was this: **it's just hair.** For so long, he had convinced himself that losing his hair would somehow make him, less attractive, less confident, less *himself*. But the reality?

Losing hair doesn't change who you are. If anything, it forces you to figure out what really matters what makes you *you*, hair or no hair.

For Aryan, that realization was freeing. It wasn't just about accepting his thinning hair, it was about letting go of the anxiety and fear that had been tied to it. He stopped obsessing over every lost strand, stopped stressing about his hairline, and started focusing on the things that actually made him feel good, like his health, his friendships, and his newfound ability to rock a slightly receding hairline with pride.

And once Aryan let go of the need to control his hair, something funny happened: his confidence came roaring back. Sure, he wasn't walking around with a lion's mane, but he was walking around with his head held high. And that? That made all the difference.

A New Routine, A New Outlook

By the time Aryan settled into his new routine, daily walks, yoga, meditation, a healthier diet, and simple, no-fuss hair care he realized something important: **balance was the key**. Balance between indulging in the things you love (pizza, Netflix binges, occasional late-night snacks) and taking care of yourself (nutritional diet, meditation, yoga classes, morning walks, scalp massages). Balance between accepting the things you can't control (genetics, aging) and making the most of what you can control (your habits, your health, your mindset).

Aryan's new routine wasn't about trying to "fix" himself.

It was about making small, sustainable changes that helped him feel better, inside and out. And yes, while his hairline wasn't exactly charging back to the frontlines, the rest of his life had improved in ways he hadn't expected.

His energy levels were higher, his stress was lower, and his overall sense of well-being had skyrocketed. Aryan might not have won the battle against genetics, but he'd found a way to thrive in spite of it. And that, in Aryan's eyes, was a victory.

The Hairline That Stayed (Mostly) in Place

So, where did Aryan end up on his hair journey?

Well, his hairline didn't miraculously regrow overnight. There was no dramatic before-and-after moment where Aryan suddenly woke up with a full head of hair, ready to star in a shampoo commercial. But here's the thing: Aryan's hairline *stabilized*. The constant shedding slowed down and stopped, his hair felt stronger and healthier, and most importantly Aryan stopped worrying about it so much.

Aryan had something much more valuable: **peace of mind**.

He wasn't fighting his hair anymore. He was taking care of it. He wasn't obsessing over every new product or worrying about what people thought of his thinning crown. He was focused on living his life, enjoying the things that mattered, and letting go of the things he couldn't control.

Aryan's outlook on life? That had completely changed.

More Than Just Hair: The Bigger Lesson

At the end of the day, Aryan's journey wasn't just about hair. It was about **acceptance**. About learning to let go of the things you can't change and focusing on the things you can. About realizing that confidence doesn't come from having a perfect head of hair (or a perfect anything, for that matter). It comes from how you feel about yourself, how you show up in the world, and how you handle the curveballs life throws your way.

Aryan learned that hair loss while annoying wasn't the crisis he once thought it would be. It was just another part of life, like getting older or finding your first gray hair. And once he stopped stressing about it, he found a new kind of freedom. Freedom from the pressure to look a certain way, freedom from the fear of losing something he couldn't control, and freedom to focus on what really mattered.

Aryan's hair journey might have started with panic, but it ended with peace. And that, my friends, is the real win.

In the end Aryan got his hair transplant and regained his hair line of youth. This was just an icing on cake. However Aryans attitude towards life had completely changed with his newly found magical triad of yoga, meditation and **45 mins** of early morning walks.

The Final Takeaway: It's All About Confidence

So, what's the moral of Aryan's story? What's the big takeaway from his hair-raising (and occasionally hilarious) journey?

Here it is: **Confidence doesn't come from your hair. It comes from how you live your life.**

Aryan learned that you don't need a full head of hair to feel good about yourself. You just need to take care of yourself physically, mentally, and emotionally. You need to find the things that make you feel strong, healthy, and happy, and focus on those. Whether it's a morning walk, meditation, a yoga class, or a pizza night with friends, the key is balance. And the key to confidence? That's being okay with who you are, hair or no hair.

Aryan's hair may have thinned due to genetics, but his confidence surged with positive approach towards life and hair transplant. He embraced a healthier lifestyle, and discovered that feeling good isn't about having the perfect appearance it's about feeling good in your own skin (or, in Aryan's case, under your own hair).

The Journey Continues...

Aryan's hair story isn't over because, let's face it, hair is a lifelong thing. There will be more good hair days, bad hair days, and everything in between. But the difference now? Aryan isn't stressing about it anymore. He's found his groove, his balance, and his confidence. And whether his hair sticks around for another few years or decides to head for the hills, Aryan knows he's going to be just fine.
Because, at the end of the day, it's not about your hair. It's about how you handle what life throws your way.

The End (but really, the beginning of Aryan's new, carefree, confident life).